TEACHERS' NIGHT BEFORE HALLOWEEN

By
Steven L. Layne

Pictures by
Ard Hoyt

PELICAN PUBLISHING COMPANY
Gretna 2008

For Lisa Owen, Elizabeth and Peter Sompolski, and for Kathleen Bruni, Marilyn Jancewicz, and Valerie Cawley—two of the finest teams of educators with whom anyone ever had the privilege to teach. Thanks for the memories.
—SLL

To my inspirational friend, Steve Layne.
—AH

The word "Pelican" and the depiction of a pelican are trademarks of Pelican Publishing Company, Inc., and are registered in the U.S. Patent and Trademark Office.

Library of Congress Cataloging-in-Publication Data

Layne, Steven L.
  Teacher's night before Halloween / by Steven L. Layne ; pictures by Ard Hoyt.
      p. cm.
   ISBN-13: 978-1-58980-585-9 (hardcover : alk. paper) 1. Halloween—Juvenile poetry. 2. Children's poetry, American. I. Hoyt, Ard, ill. II. Title.
   PS3612.A96T43 2008
   811'.6—dc22

                              2008004130

Printed in Korea
Published by Pelican Publishing Company, Inc.
1000 Burmaster Street, Gretna, Louisiana 70053

'Twas the day before Halloween
And all through the school
Teachers tried to keep order
And to not lose their cool

It was no small achievement
For as everyone knows
Halloween tops the list
Of all-time teacher woes

Kids brought costumes in early
And were trying them on
Just as soon as they saw
That the buses were gone

When the opening bell rang
Some children went wild
Well-established routines
Were completely defiled

Four grotesque fifth-grade monsters
Were preparing to dine
On two fine first-grade boys
Who'd been tied up with twine

And a second-grade teacher
Showed girls who was king

When he broke up their bathroom
Tiara trade-ring

Lindsay Lowe's party cupcakes
Arrived a day early
And when third graders heard "not today"
They grew surly

So upset was sweet Lindsay
And her two BFFs
That they passed out the treats
While Miss Smith graded tests

There was icing on desks
Cupcake sprinkles in hair
Soon the wrappers and crumbs
Could be found everywhere

Fourth grade, at first,
Was a much calmer sight
Until space rangers started
A laser sword fight

By the noon hour
The faculty lounge filled with moans
As the teachers lamented
Tomorrow's true groans

There'd be even more costumes
And a whole lot more treats
Plus the mothers with cameras
Who'd line nearby streets

For the costume parade—
A longstanding tradition
That had never successfully
Been decommissioned

"Take heart now—cheer up
We've all done this before,"
The art teacher cried
As she burst through the door

"Hey, I've got it! What fun!
And it won't be that hard
This year we'll each dress
Like a big credit card"

"The kids will just love it,"
She shouted with glee
"Now everyone meet
In my art room at three"

"Tom, you'll be a SuperCharge
MaxIt for Sue
Mrs. Hudgens, you're *Frenchy's*—
That's perfect for you!"

"Well it's better than last year,"
Mr. Anderson said
"Those Rockette boots cut blood flow
In both of my legs"

That afternoon, chaos
Fueled fears of tomorrow
The teachers' hearts filled
With great tension and sorrow

Then the principal
Issued a memo—quite strict

"No one takes the day off
And you can't call in sick!"

Principal Layne

The three o'clock meeting—
It came and it went
And the truth was the teachers
Were already spent

They filed out in silence
With their butcher-block paper
And some paints and some markers
Plus a pattern to taper

The sides of their costumes
To fit them just right
And they drove home resolved
That they'd give up the fight

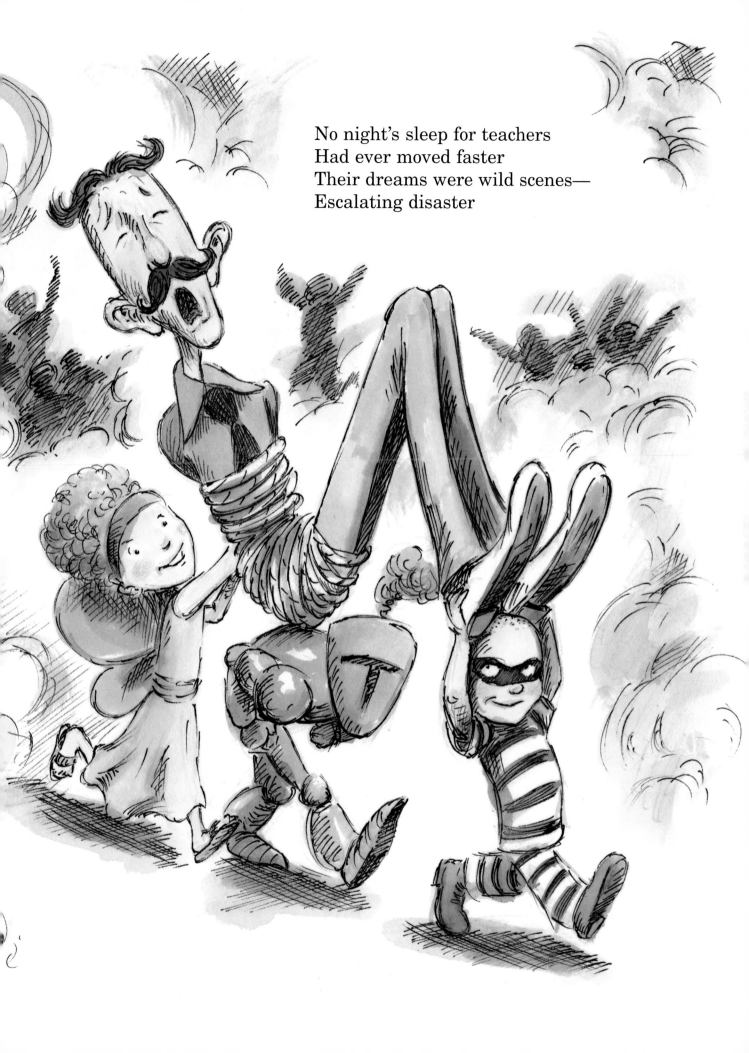

No night's sleep for teachers
Had ever moved faster
Their dreams were wild scenes—
Escalating disaster

Finally, Halloween came
As it did each school year
But this time the teachers
Had nothing to fear

On the playground that morning
A sight filled their eyes
Whether trick or a treat
It was quite a surprise

All the children looked *normal*
None had swords or grenades
There were no children dressed
Like their teachers or aides

Then the parents exclaimed
As they rushed out from hiding,
"Hooray for great teachers!
This is just so exciting!"

"The parade has been cancelled
The costumes have, too
For *just this one year*
All the treats are for you!"

"You've an extra-long lunch
And a fine catered meal
This year Halloween
Is the teachers' big deal!"

"Wait till you see dessert
It's a set of tiered cakes
And we've got a masseuse
In the lounge for your breaks."

Several teachers were speechless
This was so unexpected
Then the principal cheered,
"Halloween's been corrected!"

But the kids sideways glanced
And replied, "Have no fear
Though this Halloween's special
Look out for *next* year."

"Plans are well underway
And we won't miss a beat
Next year's Halloween
Will be more *trick* than treat!"